For Brenda

Published by Roaring Brook Press

Roaring Brook Press is a division of Holtzbrinck Publishing Holdings Limited Partnership

143 West Street, New Milford, Connecticut 06776

Distributed in Canada by H.B. Fenn and Company Ltd.

Library of Congress Cataloging-in-Publication Data

Franson, Scott E..

Un-brella / Scott E. Franson.

p. cm.

Summary: In this wordless book, a little girl uses her magic umbrella to give her the weather she wants, regardless of what the conditions really are outside..

ISBN-13: 978-1-59643-179-9   ISBN-10: 1-59643-179-2

[1. Weather—Fiction. 2. Umbrellas—Fiction. 3. Magic—Fiction.] I. Title.

PZ7.F8592458Unb 2007   [E]—dc22   2006047658

Roaring Brook Press books are available for special promotions and premiums.

For details contact: Director of Special Markets, Holtzbrinck Publishers.

Printed in China

First Edition April 2007

2 4 6 8 10 9 7 5 3 1

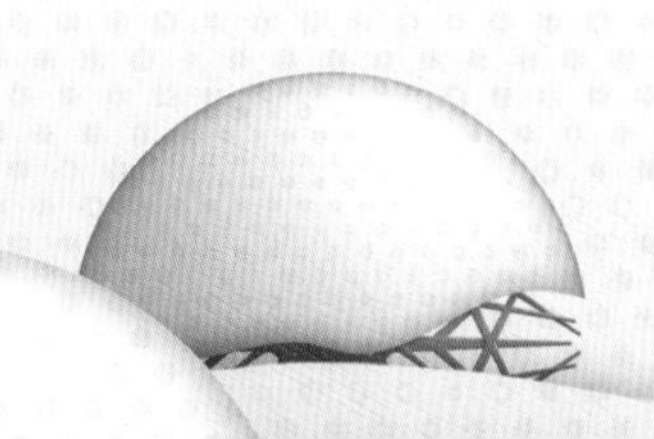

Un-Brella

Scott E. Franson

ROARING BROOK PRESS
NEW MILFORD, CONNECTICUT